Persephone and the Pomegranate

A Myth from Greece

KRIS WALDHERR

Dial Books for Young Readers New York

Pronunciation Guide

Persephone	Per-*sef*-oh-nee
Demeter	Deh-*meh*-ter
Pluto	*Ploo*-toh
Hecate	*Heh*-kah-tee
Helios	*Hee*-lee-os
Zeus	Zoose

Published by Dial Books for Young Readers
A Division of Penguin Books USA Inc.
375 Hudson Street
New York, New York 10014

Copyright © 1993 by Kris Waldherr
All rights reserved / Printed in Hong Kong
Typography by Amelia Lau Carling
First Edition
1 3 5 7 9 10 8 6 4 2

Library of Congress Cataloging in Publication Data
Waldherr, Kris.
Persephone and the pomegranate : a myth from Greece /
Kris Waldherr. — 1st ed.   p.   cm.
Summary: Demeter refuses to allow spring to appear until
she has been reunited with her daughter Persephone,
who has been abducted to the Underworld by Pluto.
ISBN 0-8037-1192-1 (lib.). — ISBN 0-8037-1191-3 (trade)
1. Persephone (Greek deity)—Juvenile literature.
[1. Persephone (Greek deity) 2. Mythology, Greek.]   I. Title.
BL820.P7W35   1993   398.21—dc20   92-21349   CIP   AC

The art for each picture consists of an oil painting.
On some of the paintings pastel dust was used.

For my mother

A long time ago, when gods and goddesses still lived among humans, Demeter, goddess of the harvest, had a daughter named Persephone whom she treasured more than the earth. Together they roamed through forests and fields as Demeter brought forth food and flowers from the soil. Persephone loved her mother's company and was rarely seen apart from her.

One day as she gathered blossoms in a distant meadow, Persephone noticed a flower unlike any other she had ever seen. It was a narcissus, so deep a red it was almost black. Its unusual color frightened her. Persephone did not pick it but instead went home. She did not tell her mother about it.

That night Persephone dreamt of the blood-red narcissus turning into a cool ripe fruit too delicious to eat. Abruptly she awoke. She slipped out of bed and ran to the meadow where she had seen the flower. The narcissus was still there, luminous in the light from the full moon. She forgot her fear and bent to pluck it.

Suddenly the earth split in two. Persephone screamed, dropping the narcissus. Out of the abyss leapt a gold chariot pulled by four black horses. Its driver, a tall man, seized Persephone by the waist and pulled her into the chariot. Down, down, they sped. Above them the earth sealed shut with a shudder.

Demeter was awakened by the echoes of her daughter's last cry. "Persephone!" she called out again and again to the calm night. But there was no answer. Demeter searched frantically until the sun rose. She did not find her daughter.

Thirteen days and nights passed. Still Demeter looked, never stopping for rest nor food. Each evening the moon waned thinner and gave off less and less light.

By the fourteenth night the moon showed her ebony face. Demeter had traveled to the far ends of the earth and waited for Hecate, goddess of the dark moon, to appear. The sky was black, as though a veil had been thrown over even the brightest stars.

After a short time a ghostly figure approached Demeter. "Sister," Hecate said, "I know why you seek my help. But I do not know where Persephone is. Perhaps Helios of the all-seeing sun can tell us."

Together Demeter and Hecate journeyed past the clouds to the top of the high mountain where Helios, the sun god, lived.

"Nothing can be done to help Persephone," Helios told Demeter. "She has been abducted by Pluto, lord of the underworld, to become his wife and rule over the dead. But Pluto does love your daughter and he is not an unworthy son-in-law."

Demeter wept, thinking of her daughter inside the earth where no sun fell nor flower grew. "Surely Zeus, ruler of us all, will help—"

"Zeus won't, Goddess. He gave Pluto permission to marry your daughter."

Demeter's sorrow quickly turned to anger. "Then I will not let the wheat grow! Let the earth be as barren as this mother's heart!"

Immediately trees began to wither and grass turned brown with death.

Deep in the underworld, surrounded by dark stone walls, Persephone sat next to Pluto on a richly jeweled throne. A heavy golden crown rested upon her brow. Pale spirits danced gracefully before the king and queen to lighten their hearts. But Persephone looked away so that no one could see her tears.

"My wife, I have given you a kingdom to rule, incomparable riches, and my love," Pluto said. "How can I please you?"

Persephone answered, "I miss my mother. I miss the sun and the green forests. I am not used to darkness, my lord."

"Still you have not eaten anything."

"Nor shall I until I am reunited with my mother," she replied.

"Perhaps this will awaken your appetite," said Pluto. He placed before Persephone a pomegranate as red and rich in color as that unearthly narcissus had been. From the fruit seeped a luscious fragrance. Tempted, Persephone held the pomegranate carefully and felt its cool surface upon her palms.

On the earth, without Demeter's guidance the trees remained barren of fruit and wheat did not grow. For the first time winter visited the earth. Ice formed on tree branches and snow covered the ground, softening the cries of hungry birds.

In her grief Demeter disguised herself as an old hag and wandered aimlessly, mourning Persephone. During her travels some recognized the goddess despite her rags. No matter how they begged her to make spring return, Demeter refused.

Zeus observed this, yet remained steadfast in his decision. But when mortal men and women began to starve, he finally surrendered to Demeter. He agreed to reunite Persephone with her mother—but only if she had not eaten.

The earth opened, allowing a brief ray of sunlight to enter the underworld before it closed once more. Even in the darkness Persephone could see the brilliant corn-gold of Demeter's hair.

"Mother!" she cried joyously as she ran into the goddess's arms. "You have come for me! I can go home with you!"

"Yes, my darling. But first," Demeter's anxious eyes searched Persephone's face, "tell me, have you eaten anything since you have been here? If you have, you must stay." Persephone said she had not, but could not meet her mother's gaze.

Pluto stepped down from his throne to take his wife's hands away from Demeter's. "Then Persephone, where is the pomegranate I gave you?"

"I know not," Persephone answered meekly.

"It must be found before you leave me. Surely you remember where it is!"

Still Persephone denied knowing. They persisted with their questions. Finally Persephone yielded the fruit from a fold in her gown. Her face was pale and nervous.

Six seeds were missing from the pomegranate.

"Persephone stays!" Pluto shouted. "She has eaten!"

"She has only tasted a few seeds," protested Demeter. "If my daughter does not return with me, I shall die of grief."

Now Persephone stepped forward. She stood between her mother and husband with a new serenity and strength.

"I shall decide this matter," she said. "True, I have eaten of the pomegranate. But, my husband, if you love me, you will understand that I am not a creature of darkness. Allow me to return to the sun and flowers I love. Allow me to leave with my mother and I will return to you six months of the year, a month for each eaten seed."

Pluto was silent. He could find little fault with Persephone's logic and he *did* love her. With sadness he allowed her to leave.

Alone, he held the pomegranate.

Over the land, snow melted into rushing brooks, carrying water to nurture new life. Ice dissolved from the trees, which began to bloom after the harsh winter. Sweet smelling flowers blossomed over fields and forests. Once again, Persephone and her mother walked through the meadows enjoying each other's company even more because of their separation.

But every year after the harvest is brought in, Persephone always remembers her promise to Pluto and returns to him. Then Demeter grieves and brings on winter. Six months later when Persephone reappears from the dark underworld, Demeter rejoices and the earth blooms again with spring.